NERO, THE CIRCUS LION

RICHARD BARNUM

NERO THE CIRCUS LION

CHAPTER I

NERO HAS SOME FUN

Far off in the jungle of Africa lived a family of lions.

Africa, you know, is a very hot country, and what we, in this land, would call a forest, or woods, is called a "jungle" there. In the jungle grew many trees, and the ground was covered with low vines and bushes so that animals, creeping along, could scarcely be seen. That was why the animals liked the jungle so much; they could roam about in it, play and get their meals, and the black hunters and the white huntsmen who sometimes came to the jungle, could not easily see to shoot the lions, elephants and other beasts.

There were five lions in this jungle family, and I am going to tell you the story of one of them, named Nero. Nero was a little boy lion, about two years old, but please don't think he was a baby because he was only two years old. Lions grow much faster than boys and girls, and a lion of two years is quite large and strong, with sharp claws and sharper teeth.

Nero lived with his father and mother, Mr. and Mrs. Lion, and his brother Chet and his sister Boo, in a cave in the African jungle. The cave was among the rocks, and not far from a spring of water where the lions went to drink each night. They drank only at night because that was the safest time; the hunters could not so easily see the shaggy lions with their big heads, and manes larger than those of a horse.

Nero was the largest of the three lion children, and he was called Nero because that always seems to be the right name for some one large and strong. Chet, who was Nero's brother, got his name because, when he was a little baby lion cub, he used to make that sound when he cried for his dinner.

As for Boo—well, I must tell you in what a funny way she got her name, and then I'll go on with the story of Nero. When Boo, who was Nero's sister, was a little baby lion, she was sitting in the front of the jungle cave one day, waiting for her mother to come back. Mrs. Lion had gone out a little way into the jungle to get something to eat.

All of a sudden Boo, who up to then had no name, heard some one coming along the jungle path, stepping on twigs and tree branches and making them crack. By this sound the little girl lion cub knew some one was coming.

"That must be my mother," thought Boo. "I'll just hide behind this piece of rock, and then I'll jump out and make believe to scare her. It will be lots of fun."

So Boo hid behind the rock near the front door of the cave-house, and, when the noise came nearer, the little girl lion jumped out and cried: "Boo!" or something that sounded very much like it.

But the little girl lion had made a mistake. Instead of her mother who was coming along the jungle path, it was a big prickly hedgehog with sharp quills all over his back, and when Boo put out her paw she was stuck full of stickery quills. The quills in a hedgehog's back are loose, and come out easily.

"Boo! Boo!" roared the little lion cub girl, but this time she was crying instead of trying to make believe scare some one. The hedgehog, however, was very much frightened—almost all the jungle animals were afraid of the lions—and this hedgehog ran away.

But the little girl lion's paw hurt her very much, and when a little later, Mrs. Lion came back, with something to eat, and found out what had happened, she said Boo had been very foolish.

And when Mr. Lion heard the story, and Nero and Chet had been told about it, they all said that "Boo" would be a very good name for the little sister lion.

"I don't care what you call me," said Boo, speaking in lion talk of course. "I don't care what my name is, if you'll only get these hedgehog stickers out of my paw."

Then they pulled the hedgehog spines out of the little girl lion's paw, and she washed it in cool water at the spring, which made her foot feel better.

For two years the lion cubs, Nero, Chet and Boo, had lived with their father and mother in the jungle cave. They learned how to tread softly on the leaves and twigs of the jungle path, so as to make no noise. They learned how to creep quietly down to the spring at night to get a drink, so that the hunters would not hear them.

All about them, in the jungle, lived other wild animals. There were several families of lions in that same part of the forest, and very often a herd of elephants would pass by, tramping and crashing their way through the jungle. The lions never bothered the elephants.

"Where are you going, Nero?" asked his mother of the lion boy cub one day, as she saw him starting out from the jungle cave. "Where are you going?"

"Oh, just out to have some fun," he answered. "I'm going to play with Switchie."

"Switchie," was the name of another lion boy cub, who lived in the cave next to Nero's. He was about a year older than the lion chap about whom I am going to tell you in this story. Switchie was called that because he switched his tail about in such a funny way.

"So you are going to play with Switchie, are you?" asked Mrs. Lion, as she looked at a place where a sharp stone had cut her foot, though the sore was now getting better. "Well, if you go to play with that lion boy don't get into mischief."

"What's mischief, Ma?" asked Nero.

"Mischief is trouble," his mother answered, speaking in lion talk, just as your dog or your cat speaks its own kind of language. "So don't get into trouble. Don't go to the spring now to get a drink, for the hunters may be watching, and may shoot you with an arrow, or with a queer lead stone, from a thing called a gun, which is worse. So don't get into mischief."

"I won't," promised Nero, and he meant to keep his word, but then he didn't count on Switchie. That chap was a bold little lion cub, larger than Nero, and always up to some trick.

"Hello, Nero!" growled Switchie, when he saw his friend coming along the jungle path.

"Hello!" growled Nero.

Now please don't imagine, just because these lions growled, that they were cross. They weren't anything of the sort. That was just their way of talking. Your dog barks and growls, and that is his way of speaking. Your cat mews and sometimes growls or "spits," and often purrs, especially when you tickle her ears. And a lion always growls when he talks. When he is angry he roars—that's the difference. And, I almost forgot, lions can purr, too, only it sounds like a buzz saw instead of the way your cat purrs. But then a lion's throat is very big, and so his purr has to be big also.

"Want to have some fun?" asked Switchie, as Nero lay down in the jungle shade.

"That's what I came over for," Nero answered. "Only my mother said I wasn't to get into any mischief."

"Oh, no, we won't do anything like that!" replied Switchie. "We'll just go along in the jungle and have some fun. I know where there is some soft grass, and we can roll over and over in that and scratch our backs."

"Fine!" said Nero. "We'll go there."

So Switchie led the way along another jungle path to a place where very few trees grew. In the midst of these few trees was a grassy place. That is, it had been green and grassy once when it was raining, which it does for several months at a time in the jungle. But the rains had stopped, the hot sun had come out from behind the clouds and dried the grass up, so that it was now like hay.

"And it's just fine to roll in. It scratches your back just hard enough," said Switchie, making his tail, with the tuft of hair on the end, swing about in a funny way.

"I like to have my back scratched," said Nero.

So the two boy lions went to have some fun and roll in the dried grass. It was just as if you had gone to roll and tumble on the hay in Grandpa's barn. The lion boys leaped about, jumped over one another, made believe bite one another and played tag with their paws.

As Switchie had said, the dried, curled grass tickled their backs just enough when they rolled over and over in it. But at last Switchie said:

"Say, aren't you thirsty?"

"Yes," answered Nero, "I am."

"Then let's go to the spring and get a drink," went on Switchie.

"Oh no! My mother said I wasn't to go to the spring in the daytime!" exclaimed Nero. "There may be hunters there, waiting to shoot us."

"Oh, I don't believe there are," said Switchie. "I'll tell you what we can do. My mother didn't tell me not to go to the spring, so I'll walk on ahead until we come to it. Then I can look and see if there are any hunters. If there aren't you can come out of the jungle and get a drink. Won't that be all right?"

"Yes, I guess it will," said Nero. "Mother wouldn't want me not to have a drink. All she's afraid of are the hunters."

"Then come on!" growled Switchie. "We'll go to the spring, and we'll have some fun on the way."

So the two boy lions walked along the jungle path to the spring where all the animals drank. On the way they fell down and rolled over and cuffed one another with their paws — the way all lions do to have fun. Nero was having a very good time, and he never gave a thought about not minding his mother.

At last Switchie and Nero came close to the spring.

"Now you stay behind this bush until I look out and see if there are any hunters," said Switchie.

"All right," answered Nero.

Carefully the older lion boy peeped through the bushes. There was no one at the spring except some little monkeys, getting a drink, and as soon as they saw the lion boy away they scampered, chattering, for the monkeys were afraid of the lions.

"Everything is all right!" called Switchie to the hiding Nero. "There are no hunters! Come on and get a drink."

Nero was very thirsty, after having played and had fun in the hot jungle sun, and he very much wanted a drink. So he rushed down to the spring, which was quite a large one, and began to lap up the water, just as your dog or cat drinks milk from a dish.

"Isn't this fun?" growled Switchie, as he stopped drinking for a moment. "Aren't we having fun, Nero?"

"Lots of fun!" answered the other lion cub.

And just then something happened. There was a rattle of the dried leaves in the jungle back of the spring. Something very hard hit Nero in the side, and a voice cried:

"There! I'll teach you to drink from my edge of the spring! Take that!"

And the next moment Nero felt himself sliding down the slippery bank of the spring, and into the water he went with a big splash!

CHAPTER II

NERO GOES HUNTING

The first thought of Nero, the little lion cub boy, as he felt himself falling into the spring of water, was that Switchie had played a joke and pushed him in.

"And when I get out I'll push him in," thought Nero. But that was all he had time to think, just then, for his head went away under the water—as the spring was deep— and Nero had to think of getting out. So he splashed and scrambled his way to shore, clawing and spluttering and half choking, for lions are not good swimmers. Indeed few animals of the cat family are, and lions belong to the cat family, you know, as do tigers and jaguars.

So, with his eyes and nose and mouth full of water, Nero scrambled to shore, a very wet and bedraggled lion boy indeed. On the shore he saw Switchie standing looking at him. Switchie was nice and dry.

"What did you do that for?" growled Nero to Switchie, as soon as our friend had shaken some of the water off his shaggy, tawny-yellow coat. "I'll fix you for that! Fun is all right, but you know I don't like jumping into the water, however much I like a drink from the spring. Now I'm going to push you in!" and Nero started to run toward Switchie.

"Hey! Wait a minute!" cried Switchie, raising his paw to push Nero away if the younger lion cub should come too near. "I didn't do anything to you."

"Yes, you did!" growled Nero. "You pushed me into the water!"

"No, I didn't!" answered Switchie. "I was taking my second drink, when I heard a noise, and I looked up and saw you sliding down into the water. But I didn't push you in."

"Who did, then?" asked Nero, looking around, quite fiercely for a little lion boy. "Who did? If I find out, I'll push him in! If it was one of the monkeys—"

"Oh, it wasn't any of them," said Switchie quickly. "They won't come near the spring when we lions are drinking."

"But it was some one!" said Nero. "I heard some one say I couldn't drink on his edge of the spring, and then I was pushed in. Who did it? I want to know that!"

9

"I did it!" said a grumbling sort of voice, and up out of the spring came something which, at first, looked like a log of wood. It was dark, and had knobs, or warts, on it, as has the trunk of a tree.

"Who—who are you?" asked Nero, in surprise. "Are you a log of wood that can speak?"

"Look out! Gracious no! That's a crocodile!" cried Switchie. "I forgot about their being here. Come on! Run!"

And as Nero saw what he had thought was a log of wood open a big mouth with many sharp teeth in it, the little lion boy ran after Switchie, who scampered off along the jungle path as fast as he could go.

"What's the matter? What was that thing which looked like a log floating in the water?" asked Nero, when he and Switchie stopped to rest in the shadow of a big tree.

"That's a crocodile, I told you!" said Switchie. "They are very big and strong, and if they get hold of your soft and tender nose, when you are drinking at the pool, they can pull you under water and drown you. You want to be careful about crocodiles."

"Well, I will," said Nero. "Only I didn't know about them before. Was it the crocodile who knocked me into the water?"

"Yes," answered Switchie, "it was. A crocodile has a long and very strong tail, with knobs and sharp ridges on it. They can knock you into the water with their tail, and then they bite you. I didn't know there were crocodiles at our spring, or I wouldn't have gone there in the daytime for a drink. At night it's all right, for then they can't see you so plainly."

"Well, this one saw me all right," said Nero. "My side is sore where he knocked me into the spring."

"It's lucky your nose isn't sore where he might have bitten you," growled Switchie. "That was a mean crocodile! We had just as good right to drink on that side of the spring-pool as he had!"

"Well, maybe we had," said Nero. "But he was stronger than I, and so he knocked me in. Now I'm all wet!"

And so Nero learned one of the first lessons of the jungle, that it is the strongest and fiercest animals that have the best of it.

The elephants of the jungle, which are the largest animals, crash their way through, afraid of nothing except the men hunters. And the lions, when the elephants are not near, are the real kings of the jungle. Few animals stay to drink at the spring when the lion roars, to say he is coming.

But this was in daylight and Switchie and Nero were only lion cubs, so, I suppose, the crocodile was not afraid of them. And, being big and strong, he just knocked Nero into the water, and claimed that as his side of the pool, though he had no right to.

"Come on," said Switchie to Nero, after they had gone a little way further through the jungle and back from the spring. "Come on; I know how we can have some more fun."

"No, I've had enough for to-day," said Nero. "I'm going home and lie down in the cave. My side hurts where the crocodile struck me with his tail."

"Oh, come on! Play tag!" begged Switchie.

"No," said Nero. "I'm going home."

And home he went. As soon as his mother saw him, wet and muddy as he still was, Mrs. Lion said:

"Well, Nero, what happened to you? Did you get into mischief?"

"I don't know, Ma," answered Nero. "But I got in the spring!"

"There! I told you to keep away from the water hole in the daytime!" said Mrs. Lion. "I knew something would happen if you played with that Switchie. That lion cub will get into trouble some day. He is too bold!"

"A crocodile knocked me into the water," explained Nero. "It wasn't Switchie's fault."

"It was the fault of both you lion boys for going where you ought not to," said Nero's mother. "Now you see what happened. But I'm sorry your side is hurt. Go into the cave and lie down. I'll bring you a nice piece of goat meat to eat, and get some soft grass to make you a bed. You'll be all right in a few days, but after this — mind me!"

"I will," promised Nero.

The soft grass, which his mother pawed into a bed for him with her sharp claws, felt very comfortable to his sore side. And the goat's meat, which lions eat when they can get it, tasted very good. Nero soon became dry and then he went to sleep.

When he awakened his brother Chet and his sister Boo were in the cave looking at him.

"Mother says you got into mischief!" exclaimed Boo. "Tell us all about it, Nero."

So Nero did, and when his story was ended Chet said enviously:

"I wish I had been there. If I had, I'd have scratched that crocodile with my claws!"

"You couldn't have hurt him that way," said Mr. Lion, who came into the cave just then. "Crocodiles have a very hard, thick skin on their backs and tails, much harder and thicker than our skin, and even that of an elephant. You can't hurt a crocodile by scratching his back. The only way to hurt them is to turn them over, and while you are trying to do that they'll knock you about with the big tail. So keep away from the crocodiles, children."

"I will," said Nero, and Boo and Chet said the same thing.

"Now hurry and get well," said Nero's father to him, as the lion boy lay in the cave. "You are growing large and strong, and soon you will have to learn to go hunting."

"What's hunting?" asked Nero.

"It is learning how to get your own things to eat," said his father. "When you were little, your mother and I hunted the goats and other animals that we have to eat. But now you are getting big enough to go hunting for yourself. Only I must give you a few lessons."

"Can't I learn to hunt, too?" asked Chet.

"And I?" Boo wanted to know.

"Yes," said their father. "After I teach Nero I'll teach you. One at a time. The jungle is full of danger, and I can teach only one of you at a time how to be careful. So get good and well and strong, Nero, and soon I'll take you on a hunt."

Nero thought he would like this, so he stayed quietly in the cave for a day or two, until his side, where the crocodile had struck him with the sharp-ridged tail, felt much better.

One day, about a week after Nero had been tossed into the spring, he noticed his father sharpening his claws on the bark of a tree.

"What's he doing that for?" Nero asked his mother.

"To get ready for the jungle hunt to-night," answered Mrs. Lion. "I heard him say something about taking you, so perhaps you had better sharpen your claws, also."

"I will," answered Nero, and he did, making the bits of bark fly as he pulled it from a tree in the jungle, not far from the cave where he lived.

When it began to get dark, which it does very early in the big African forest, as the thick trees shut out the light of the sun, Nero said to his mother:

"Aren't we going to have any supper?"

"Not to-night—that is, not right away," said Mr. Lion. "You are going to hunt for your supper, Nero."

"But I am very hungry," returned the little lion boy, who was growing bigger and stronger every day.

"Then you will hunt all the better," growled his father. "There is nothing like being hungry to make a good hunter-lion. Come, now is the time I have long waited for— to teach you to hunt in the jungle. Your mother and Chet and Boo are going to have supper with Switchie and his folks. You and I are going to hunt for ourselves. Come, we will go into a part of the jungle where you have never yet been."

And Nero felt very much excited when he heard his father say this. The lion cub felt brave and strong, and he knew that his teeth and claws were very sharp.

Suddenly, through the jungle, which was now quite dark, there came a distant sound as if of thunder. There was a rumble and a roar, and the very ground seemed to shake.

"What's that?" asked Nero, looking at his father.

CHAPTER III

NERO IS SHOT

Once again, as Nero stood with Mr. Lion at the front door of the jungle cave, the roaring sound echoed among the trees.

"What is that?" asked the boy lion once more.

"That is the roaring of other lions, who are also going out to hunt to-night," said Nero's father. "There will be many of us lions in the jungle; perhaps others, like you, who are going out for the first time. You must be brave and strong. Remember the lessons your mother and I have taught you. Crouch down and jump hard. Strike hard with your paws and dig deep with your sharp claws. That is what they are for—to help you hunt so that you may get things to eat. Now we will start."

By this time the jungle around the cave where Nero lived seemed filled with the roarings of other lions. The very ground seemed to tremble. Nero was excited, but he was sure he could hunt well. He was a brave lion, and he knew he was strong and nearly full grown now, and he knew his teeth were sharp, as were his claws, and his paws were strong, both for striking and leaping, for that is how a lion hunts.

"Boom! Boom!" rolled out the lions' roars in the jungle.

"Ah, we shall have a grand hunt to-night!" said Nero's father. "I hope you are still hungry."

"Yes I am, very," answered the boy lion.

"That is good," returned the father. "Now we will start. At first stay close to me, but when you see a goat or a sheep or some other animal you think you would like to eat, spring on it and strike it with your claws."

Of course this sounds cruel, but lions must get their food this way; there is no other.

Suddenly Nero opened his mouth and gave a great roar, the loudest he had ever uttered. It shook the ground on which he stood. The trembling of the earth seemed to tickle the pads of skin and flesh of his paws, pads which were the same to him as your shoes are to you.

"Ha, that was a fine roar, Nero!" said his father. "Roar again!"

And Nero did, louder than at first.

"That's the way!" cried Mr. Lion. "That will tell the other jungle folk to keep out of our way when we are having a night-hunt."

And that, I suppose, is why lions roar. They do it to frighten away the other animals who might spoil their hunt in the jungle.

For the lion's voice, when he roars, is frightfully loud. There is no other animal who can make so much noise—not even the elephant, which is larger than ten lions. If you have ever heard a lion roar, even in his circus cage, or in a city park, you will never forget it.

And so Nero roared, and his father roared, and the other lions, all about them in the jungle, roared until there was a regular lion chorus, and the other beasts, hearing it, slunk back to their dens or caves, or crouched under fallen trees, and one after another said to himself:

"The lions are out hunting to-night. It is best for us to stay in until they have finished. Then it will be our turn."

And so you see how it is that the strength of a lion makes the other animals afraid when the big animals hunt. Elephants do not need to fear lions, for the big animals, with trunks and tusks, do not eat the same kind of food lions eat. Elephants live on grass, hay, palm-nuts and things that grow. But the lion eats only meat, and he would eat an elephant if he could get one, though it might take him a long while.

"Now for the hunt!" said Mr. Lion, as he led Nero into the jungle. "Tread softly. Sniff with your nose until you smell something worth hunting, and then spring on it."

Though lions, like cats, can see pretty well in the dark, they have to depend a great deal in their hunting on what they can smell with their nose, just as your dog can smell a bone, and tell, in that way, where he has buried it in the garden.

So Nero and his father joined the other lions on their march through the jungle in search of something to eat. And Nero kept getting hungrier and hungrier, so that he looked eagerly around every side of him in the darkness, and sniffed so that he might know when he came near anything he could kill and eat.

The other lions were doing the same thing. They did not roar now, but went quietly, slinking through the jungle as quietly as your cat creeps through the grass when she is trying to catch a sparrow. The lions had done enough roaring to scare away other animals who might bother them in their hunt. Now they did not roar any longer, for they did not want to scare away the smaller beasts which were food for them in their hunger.

"I'm going to leave you for a while now, Nero," said Mr. Lion, after a bit. "You will have to get along by yourself. But don't forget the lessons your mother and I taught you."

"Where are you going?" asked Nero.

"I am going to the front, to march along with the older men lions," said Nero's father. "We are going to lead you young lions where there will be good hunting."

"I shall like that," growled Nero, and he sprang on a tree trunk as he passed, and dug deep into the soft bark.

"Hi! Quit that! You're scattering bark in my eyes!" said a voice behind Nero. It was not a loud voice, for one has to be quiet when hunting in the jungle.

"Who's there?" asked Nero, thinking for a moment it might be the crocodile who had tossed him into the jungle pool.

"It is I—Switchie," was the answer.

"Oh, are you hunting, too?" asked Nero, glad to find that he knew some one among the lions besides his father. "Have you killed anything yet?"

"No, not yet. But I shall pretty soon," answered Switchie. "This isn't my first hunt. I've been out at night before."

"Isn't it great!" said Nero. "I hope I can kill a big buffalo. That would make a fine meal!"

"Yes, I should say it would!" exclaimed Switchie. "But you had better leave the buffaloes to your father and the other big men lions. They always take them. It takes a big lion to catch a buffalo, and even then sometimes the buffaloes kill a lion."

"How?" asked Nero.

"With their sharp horns," answered Switchie. "Buffaloes have terribly sharp horns. Better look out for them. Better stick to the goats and the sheep, or even a rabbit, until you learn more about hunting. As for me, I am old enough now to try for a buffalo, I think. So if you see one, tell me, and I'll kill it and give you some."

"Well, I guess I'm nearly as big and strong as you," growled Nero. "If I see a buffalo I'll jump on his back, and strike him with my paw."

"All right. But if you get hurt don't say I didn't tell you to be careful," warned Switchie. "Now come on! We must hurry or we shall be left behind. Ho for the jungle hunt!"

The two boy lions hurried on after the others. Ahead of them they could hear, faintly, the tread of the older beasts as they walked along, looking for something to strike and kill, to stop the terrible hunger. The lions only went on a hunt when they wanted something to eat. They did not kill for fun. It was their way of getting a living.

Suddenly, up in front, there sounded a crash among the tangled vines, bushes and trees of the jungle. Then came a roar, but not a very loud one.

"What's that?" asked Nero of Switchie.

"Oh, that isn't any thing. Don't be afraid," answered the other lion.

"I'm not afraid!" said Nero. "Only, I want to learn things. I never hunted in the jungle at night before, and I don't know so much about it as you do. What was that noise?"

"Oh," said Switchie, easily, "that, I suppose, was my father, or yours, killing some big animal. Maybe it was a buffalo. We'll soon find out."

And the two boy lions did. As they came to an open place in the jungle they saw Nero's father and that of Switchie crouching near something big and black lying on the ground. Off to one side was a lion, licking, with his big red tongue, a sore place on his leg.

"What happened?" asked Nero quickly, of his father.

"We killed a buffalo, Cruncher and I," said Mr. Lion, as he nodded toward Switchie's father, whose name was Cruncher. "We killed a buffalo, but my cousin, Chaw, is hurt. The buffalo stuck him with one of his horns. Then I struck down the buffalo. Here, Nero, is a bit of meat for you, and, Switchie, you may have some. But not much. This meat belongs to Cruncher and me. We will give you a little, but, if you want any more, you must hunt for yourselves. I fed you when you were a little baby lion, Nero, but now that you are big you must learn to feed and hunt for yourself."

And this, too, is the law of the jungle.

Switchie and Nero eagerly ate the bits of meat the older lions gave them, and then the hunt went on. Nero was still very hungry, and so was Switchie, and pretty soon Nero saw a small animal creeping along through the jungle.

"Ah, you are trying to get away from me!" thought Nero, who had gone to one side, and away from the others. "But I'll get you!"

Then he stalked, or crept softly after, the animal, which was a big rabbit, and, all of a sudden, Nero leaped and caught the smaller beast.

"At last I have hunted for myself!" thought Nero, as he ate his meal. "This is great! But it is not enough. I must have more!"

He went farther on in the jungle, and, all at once, he heard a goat bleating.

"Baa-a-a-a! Baa!" bleated the goat.

"Ha! There is something else I can catch for my supper!" thought Nero. "I am getting to be quite a hunter!"

By this time he was far off from his father and the other lions. But he did not mind that. He felt sure he could find his way back when he needed to.

"But first I'll catch that goat," said Nero.

Carefully he stalked through the jungle, coming nearer and nearer to where he could hear the goat bleating. At last, in an open place in the jungle, where the moon shone brightly, Nero saw the goat, a white one. It seemed caught fast in a vine, and could not move.

"Ah, I can easily get this fellow!" thought the boy lion.

He crouched for a spring, and was just going to leap through the air and on the back of the goat when, suddenly, there was a loud sound, like a small clap of thunder, and at once Nero felt a sharp pain in one paw. He rolled over and over, howling and roaring in pain and anger.

At the same time a man hidden on a platform built up in a tree, cried out:

"Oh, I have shot a lion! I have shot a lion!"

CHAPTER IV

NERO IN A CAVE

Now while the hunter, hidden on a platform in a tree in the jungle, was shouting about having shot a lion, Nero was doing some shouting of another sort. To tell the truth, he was howling and roaring, just as, sometimes, when you step on the puppy's tail, by mistake, of course, the puppy howls. Nero was howling and roaring with pain.

"Oh, what has happened? What is the matter?" cried Nero, in lion talk, of course, as he rolled over and over on the dried leaves of the jungle. "What a terrible pain in my paw! Oh, I wonder if the goat did this! If he did—"

Nero stopped his howling long enough to try to stand up and look through the jungle trees to where he had first seen the goat.

There the bleating animal was. It had not moved.

"Surely that goat couldn't have given me the pain in my paw," said Nero, between his howls. "I wonder what the goat means by staying in one place so long, especially when it must know we lions are out on a night-hunt. And what gave me the pain in my foot, and what made the loud noise?"

As Nero roared, so the other hunting lions roared. Switchie and the smaller lions, like Nero, could not roar very loudly, but Nero's father, and the other full-grown beasts made the very ground tremble with their rumblings.

At the same time there were other jungle cries from other animals. The monkeys, who had been sleeping in the tree-tops, began to chatter and scold, as they swung to and fro.

"What's the matter? What's the matter?" asked one gray-haired monkey, who must have been very old. "What's all the noise about? It reminds me of the time a monkey named Mappo, who once visited here, had the toothache one night and howled until morning. Some of you monkeys howl just like Mappo did, though he was a merry chap most of the time."

"Where is Mappo now?" asked a small baboon, which is another kind of monkey.

"Oh," replied the gray-haired chap, "Mappo went to a far country on a trip, and had many wonderful adventures. He joined a circus, and was put in a book."

"The lions are on a night-hunt," said a middle-sized monkey, who climbed down a tree to take a look. "The lions are hunting, and one of them seems to be hurt, by the way he howls."

"Very likely," said the old monkey. "I thought I heard a gun. That means hunters are about. I saw some of them in the jungle to-day, but I kept out of sight. Well, if hunters are hunting and lions are hunting, we monkeys had better stay up in the trees."

And the monkeys did. But of course that did not make the pain in Nero's foot any better. The lion boy howled and roared by turns, and with his big, rough, red tongue, he licked the place where his paw hurt. That is the only way lions have of making well their sore places; by licking them with their tongues or letting cold water run on the hurt place. But just then there was no water where Nero could get it.

"What's the matter with you, Nero?" roared the voice of Mr. Lion through the black jungle. "What are you howling about?"

"Oh, I'm hurt!" said the lion boy. "I saw a goat and tried to jump on it. Then I heard some little thunder, and my paw hurt and the goat is still there."

"Ha! That was a trap!" cried Mr. Lion. "That goat was tied there to a tree by a rope, so he would bleat and make you come closer. Then a hunter, hidden in a tree, must have shot you."

And this is exactly what had happened. The hunter knew that a lion would come close to try to catch the tied goat, when it bleated, and the man waited.

Then, when the man, hiding on a platform built in a tree, saw Nero, as the moon shone now and then, he fired his big rifle. But he did not kill a lion, as he thought. He only made Nero lame in one paw, and as the lion boy rolled away as quickly as he could the man lost sight of him. And though he and some other hunters who were with him tried later to find Nero, they could not. He had run away; and I will tell you how he did it.

"Come, lions!" called Nero's father to the hunting band, when Nero had told what had happened to him. "Come, we must not hunt here any longer. If one hunter shot Nero, other hunters may shoot at us. We had better hunt somewhere else. Come, we will run away. The jungle is big enough for us to hide from the hunters. But, before we go, we will give a loud roar so the hunters will know we are not afraid. All ready now, my brothers. Roar! Roar! Roar!"

And how those lions roared! You could have heard them a mile away, for they all roared at once, and the ground fairly trembled. Even Nero, hurt as he was, helped in the roaring.

"Come on now, Nero! Follow us!" called Mr. Lion to the boy cub who was shot. "You will have to run on three legs, but you have done that before. You did it once when you got a big thorn in your paw. Come along, follow us and we will hunt in another part of the jungle."

So the lion band turned away from the place where the goat was tied and where the hunters were hidden, and Nero followed. But it was not easy for the cub lion, and soon he began to limp and fall behind.

"What's the matter?" asked Switchie, as he saw that his chum was not keeping up with the rest. "Can't you run along faster?"

"No, I can't," answered Nero. "And I guess you couldn't either, on only three legs."

"Well, maybe I couldn't," replied Switchie. "I'm sorry you were shot, Nero. I'll stay behind and walk with you. Then you won't be lonesome."

"Thank you," answered Nero, using lion talk, of course.

So Switchie stayed behind with Nero, going slowly, as the wounded lion had to go. But soon the others—the big and little lions who were not hurt began to get far ahead.

"Come on, Nero! Come on!" they roared. "And you too, Switchie! Come along here! Hurry up!"

"I'll just run on ahead and see what they want," said Switchie to Nero. "I'll tell them you can't go fast, and that they must wait for us. I'll run up ahead and tell them this, and then come back here to you."

"All right, thank you, I wish you would," growled Nero, and he did not feel very happy, for his paw hurt him very much. "I'll wait here for you," he said, as he sat down on a pile of leaves.

So Switchie ran on ahead to tell the others. But while he was gone something happened that changed Nero's whole life, and really was the cause of his going to a circus.

I'll tell you about it.

As Nero sat on the pile of leaves, waiting for his friend Switchie to come back, he suddenly heard a noise in the jungle behind him. He saw some lights flashing and he heard the sound of talk. It was the voices of men — the same sort of voice that had shouted:

"I have shot a lion!"

Nero pricked up his ears and listened as hard as he could.

"Those are hunters!" said the boy lion to himself. "They are coming after me! I must run away and hide! I can't wait for Switchie to come back! I must hide!"

As I have said, the moon now and then shone in the jungle, making it light enough for men to see to shoot. But the lights Nero saw flashing were not moonbeams. They came from lanterns carried by the hunters.

"Here is a mark where a lion has been!" cried one hunter, flashing his light. "This must be the one I shot! Come on, we'll get him yet!"

And these were the voices Nero heard. The wounded lion boy did not wait any longer. Up he sprang, and, running on three legs, and making no noise, off through the dark jungle he hurried. His only idea was to get away and hide.

Suddenly Nero saw a blacker patch in the half darkness. He knew at once what it was. It was the opening, or front door, of a cave.

"It isn't the cave where I live," thought the lion boy, "but it will do very well for me to hide in."

So Nero crawled into the cave with his sore paw, and lay down on some dried grass, as far back as he could get. And the hunters, with their guns and lanterns, came on through the jungle, looking for a lion to kill.

CHAPTER V

NERO IN A TRAP

Tramp, tramp, tramp came the hunters through the jungle, flashing their lights and looking for the lion which one of them had shot while the hunter was hidden on the platform in a tree. But Nero, cowering away back in the dark cave, kept very still and quiet, and he heard the hunters walk right past his hiding place.

"Good!" thought the boy lion. "They haven't found me! I'm all right so far; but I wonder how long I will have to stay here, and what the other lions will do."

Poor Nero felt sick and in pain, and he was lonesome. It's as bad, I think, for a jungle lion to be this way as it would be for your dog. But still Nero did not dare come out of the cave for fear of the hunters.

"I'll just have to stay here," thought Nero, "until it's safe to come out. Guess I might as well go to sleep."

So Nero curled up on the dried grass in the cave. He knew some other lion once must have used the same cave for a sleeping place, as the grass bed was made up just as Nero's was in the home cave.

"It's a good thing I found this place," thought Nero. "But I wish my father and mother and Chet and Boo were here with me. Yes, and I even wish Switchie were here. I wonder what he is doing!"

And so, wondering, Nero fell asleep in the jungle cave. How long he slept he did not know, for it was as dark as night in the cavern, no matter whether or not the sun shone outside, and Nero was far back from the front door of the cave. When Nero awakened he tried to stand up and walk.

But the moment he put his sore paw down on the stone floor of the cave, he felt such a pain that he let out a howl and then a roar. But as soon as he had done this he knew he had better keep quiet.

"For the hunters may be around the cave yet, outside, and may hear me," thought Nero. "But, oh, how my foot hurts!"

And indeed it did, for it was all swelled up because of the bullet that had gone in from the hunter's gun. Nero could not step on his paw, and he had to limp around on three legs.

"I can't go out of the cave while I'm this way," he thought. "I could not run very fast through the jungle, and if the hunters were to see me, lame as I am, they surely would catch me."

Nero knew something about the hunters in the African jungle, for he had often heard his father and the other lions talk about the men with guns. Some of the older lions had even been shot at, and one or two of them had scars on them, to show where the bullets had gone in. But the shot places had healed. And among the stories the older lions told when they came to the cave where Nero lived, were tales of lion friends who had gone out on jungle hunts and had never returned.

"What happened to them?" Nero asked one day.

"Oh, I suppose some of them were killed dead by a gun," said old Bounder, a toothless lion who could chew only soft scraps of meat. "Others must have been caught in traps and taken away."

And Nero thought of this talk as he licked his sore paw in the jungle cave. What had happened to him was exactly like what had happened to some of the lions Bounder used to know.

"But I am still here," thought Nero; "and when my father or Switchie comes to find me they will know what has happened to me. But I wish they would hurry!"

Nero hopped on three legs about the cave. He was very thirsty, as all animals are after a meal and a sleep, and, besides, he was hot and feverish from his hurt paw. He wanted a drink very much.

Now, when a wild animal wants a drink of water he does not do as you boys and girls can do — go to a faucet or the pump and get a drink. Lions in the jungle can't get water whenever they want it, and the only way they have of telling where some may be — that is unless they live near a spring or a pool — is by smelling.

And so Nero began sniffing to see if he could smell water in the cave, as he knew he dared not go outside. And pretty soon, to his delight, he caught the sweet smell of a spring. He walked in the direction from which the smell came, and soon he heard the trickle of water. And, a little later, he came to a small spring in the far end of the cave. There was a little pool of water, and Nero took a big drink. Then he let some of the cool water run on his paw, and this made the hurt place feel better.

Nero's foot was so sore that he could not go out of the cave for two days, for it was all he could do to limp around in the cavern and get drinks of water. He dared not go outside. And in these two days he became very hungry, so that at last he felt that he must go out and see if he could not find some meat to eat.

Very carefully he poked his head outside the cave. The sun was shining brightly in the jungle, and it was nice and warm. Nero looked this way and that for a sign of a hunter, but he saw none. Then, a little distance off, he saw a small animal eating some leaves.

"There is my dinner if I can only get it," said Nero to himself. "I must try and see how much of a hunter I shall make on three legs."

Carefully, as he had been taught by his father and mother, and as he had done on the night of the big hunt when he had been hurt, Nero began to creep toward the small animal. And he caught it, too, in spite of his sore paw.

"Now I feel better!" said Nero, after his meal. "I think it will be all right to stay out of the cave for a while. I can get along better than at first, and the hunters do not seem to be around here. I'll go to the home cave now, and I'll have a great story to tell the others."

But Nero was not going to find it as easy to get home through the jungle as he had hoped. In the first place, he did not know his way, and, in the second place, he had to go very slowly. For his paw, though it was getting better, was not well yet, and sometimes, when he knocked it against a stone or a tree, it pained him so that he would have to sit down and rumble and roar and howl. But he did not howl very loudly, for this might have brought the hunters, who, he feared, might try to shoot him again.

As I have said, Nero did not know his way back home through the jungle. It had been dark when he started out with his father on the night-hunt, and he had not noticed the way they had slunk along. Then, too, Nero expected his father would be with him to show him the way back. But something had happened, as you know, to make everything different. And when Nero ran away from the hunters, and hid in the cave, he had gone farther and farther away from his own folks and home, though, at the time, he did not know it.

"If only I can get back to my own cave I'll be all right," thought the lion boy. "I must try as hard as I can to find my cave. And how I do wish I could see my father and mother, and Boo and Chet!"

So Nero wandered to and fro in the jungle, now and then stopping to drink from a pool or a spring, and when he was hungry he hunted small animals, that he could easily catch. He did not dare to go after big animals when his paw was so sore.

"If I should see a buffalo now, I'd have to run away from him," thought Nero. "But when I get well, and bigger and stronger, I'll jump on a buffalo's back, just as my father did!"

So Nero wandered on and on in the jungle, but he did not find the home cave for which he was looking. Here and there wandered the boy lion, always hoping that he might find some animal path that would lead him home. But he did not. Day after day passed, and Nero was no nearer home than at first.

Then he began to know what had happened.

"I am lost!" he thought. "I have lost my way. I must ask some of the jungle animals how to get home."

But this was not easy. Most of the jungle animals were afraid of the lion, though he was not yet full grown, and when he roared at them, to ask where his cave was, they thought he was trying to scare them or catch them, and they ran away.

The larger animals, like the elephants, who went about in herds, and who were not afraid of one lion who was all alone, did not bother to answer Nero, or else they said they knew nothing of his home.

"Do you know where I live?" asked poor, lost Nero of the monkeys he saw hopping about in the trees. "Where is my home cave? And where are Boo and Chet?"

"We don't know," answered the monkeys. "All we know is that we sit in the trees and eat coconuts when we can get them. We never saw your cave, and, besides, we don't like lions, anyhow."

Poor Nero did not know what to do, so he wandered on, eating when he could, and drinking when he came to a pool or a spring.

"If I could only meet some other lions one of them would take me home," he thought.

But the part of the jungle where Nero now was did not seem to have any lions in it except himself. By this time his paw was nearly well, and he could run about almost as fast as at first.

Once Nero came to a spring when he was very thirsty, and, as he was drinking, having driven away a lot of monkeys who were taking up the water in their paws and sipping it, all at once he felt himself knocked over as he had been knocked by the crocodile that time.

"Here! Who's doing that?" asked Nero, as he got up from the dust, where he had been knocked. "Who did that?"

"I did!" answered a loud voice, and, looking toward the spring, Nero saw an animal the color of an elephant, but not half as large. And on the end of his nose, or snout, the animal had two sharp horns, not as long, though, as the tusks of an elephant.

"Oh, so you knocked me away from the spring, did you?" asked Nero.

"Yes, I did," was the answer. "Don't you know better than to drink before me?"

"Who are you?" asked Nero.

"I am the two-horned rhinoceros," was the answer. "And the only jungle folk who can drink with me, or before me, are the elephants. A hippopotamus can, too, as a hippo, which is his short name, is a friend of mine. But, as they live in the water nearly all the time, they don't have to come to a jungle pool to drink. I had a friend once, named Chunky. He was a happy hippo, and he and I used to drink together."

"What became of him?" asked Nero. He was not angry with the rhinoceros for having knocked him away from the water. That was the law of the jungle, just as Nero had driven away the monkeys.

"What became of Chunky? Oh, he ran away and joined a circus, I believe," answered the rhinoceros.

"What's a circus?" Nero wanted to know.

"Oh, please don't bother me," replied the two-horned animal. "I am too thirsty to talk," and he drank a lot of water. Then, when he went away, it was Nero's turn. And after the lion had quenched his thirst he thought of asking the rhinoceros the way to the lost cave. But the rhinoceros was gone.

"I guess I'll have to find my own way home," thought poor Nero, as he wandered on and on in the jungle.

Several weeks passed, and though Nero grew bigger and stronger, he was still a lion cub. And he was very lonesome and homesick, because he could not find his cave. Then, one day, something happened—something very important.

Nero was very hungry, not having been able to get anything to eat for a long time, when, all at once, he smelled something good. It was meat—just what he wanted—and, looking along a jungle path used by wild animals, he saw, lying on a pile of leaves, a chunk of goat flesh.

"Ah, there is a meal for me!" thought Nero, and then, his paw being well again, he gave a spring, and landed right on the meat.

But something very strange happened. Nero suddenly felt himself falling down. Down and down he went, into a big hole, and the meat and the pile of leaves went with him. Down into a black pit fell Nero, and, as he toppled in, a black African man shouted:

"Ha! The lion is in the trap! The lion is in my trap!"

CHAPTER VI

NERO IN A CIRCUS

Nero did not know what had happened to him, except that he had fallen down into a big hole dug in the earth. He did not know what the black African man said about being in a "trap," for though Nero could understand lion talk, he did not yet know much about the talk of men. Later on he was to learn a little about that. Just now he was frightened and hurt, for when he fell down the hole he had struck his paw that had the bullet in it, and, though the sore was healed, it still pained a bit at times.

"I wonder what can have happened to me," thought Nero, as he tumbled and twisted about on the bottom of the pit, which was partly filled with dried leaves. "I wonder what this is, anyhow!"

More than once, when a very little lion boy and out walking along the jungle paths with his father and mother, Nero had fallen into a mud puddle or other hole, because he had not yet learned to walk steadily and carefully. But at such times he had easily scrambled out of the hole, or his mother had helped him.

Now Mrs. Lion was not here to do this, and, try as he did, Nero could not get out of this hole. It was too deep, and the sides were too straight. Nero tried hard enough, jumping up and clawing at the dirt, some of which got into his eyes, but jump though he did, and roar though he did, he could not get out.

Up on top, at the edge of the hole, the black African man was jumping about, waving his hands, in one of which was a long, sharp spear, and the African was shouting:

"I have caught a lion! I have a lion in my hole-trap! Whoop-la!"

Of course Nero did not know what all this meant. All he knew was that a man had something to do with his trouble.

"Maybe that is the hunter man who shot me," thought Nero; "and now he has caught me because I ran away from him and hid in the cave. Well, he has caught me at last, unless I can get out of this hole."

But Nero was wrong. This was not the same man who had shot him. This was another man, a trapper of wild animals, and he had dug a deep hole along a jungle path where he knew lions and other animals would walk. Then he covered the hole with little sticks and leaves, so they would easily break if a big animal, like Nero, jumped on them.

And that is just what Nero had done. He saw the piece of meat on the ground, and jumped straight for it. But he landed in the middle of the sticks and leaves, and fell into the hole.

That is how Nero was caught, and he did not like it at all. He wanted to be loose, to roam through the jungle as he liked. He wanted to try to find his father and his mother and Chet and Boo. But they were far away.

And, while I think of it, I might tell you that for a long time after Nero was lost, that night of the hunt, Mr. Lion looked everywhere for the boy lion. But Nero could not be found, and his father and mother and the other lions thought he had been killed by the hunters. They never saw him again, and, for a time, felt very sad. But so many things happened in the jungle that Mr. and Mrs. Lion soon forgot Nero. That's the way with animals. They are not like us. And so it was that Nero's father and mother never really knew what happened to him. They might find out if they could read this book, but that, of course, can't be done.

Now we'll get back to Nero. There he was in the bottom of a big hole, and up at the top was the black African trapper looking down on him. Pretty soon other hunters and trappers came to see the lion that had been caught alive.

"He's a fine big fellow, Chaki," said one black man to the trapper who had been so pleased when Nero was caught. "What are you going to do with him?"

"Oh, I am going to sell him to a white animal man who comes from across the sea in a big boat called a ship," answered Chaki, the trapper.

"And what will the white animal man do with a live lion?"

"He buys him to sell to a circus," answered Chaki.

"And what is a circus?" asked the other black man.

"I don't know," answered Chaki, "except that far across the ocean white people like to pay money to look at wild animals such as we have in our jungle. That's all I know about a circus. The white animal man told me that."

"Ha! A circus!" laughed the other black man. "And people pay money to look at wild animals? Well, they should come to the jungle. They could see all the animals they want for nothing."

And of course we could, I suppose, only very few of us can go to jungles, and so we go to circuses instead.

Nero, down on the bottom of the hole, listened to the talk of the black men up above. He did not understand any of it, or he might have remembered that word "circus." The rhinoceros, who had knocked him away from the drinking pool, had spoken of a "circus" where Chunky, the happy hippo, went. But Nero was too frightened and in too much pain to pay any heed to what the men said.

And then began a very unhappy time for our lion friend. It was such an unhappy, sad time that I am not going to tell you very much about this part of Nero's life. I'm going to skip over it and come to the funnier, happier part.

For, after the lion had thrashed about on the bottom of the pit for some time, the black African trapper let down ropes and tangled the lion all up in them. Then Nero was hauled to the top of the pit and put into a big wooden cage. He tried to get out, by striking the bars with his paws, and biting them with his teeth, but they were too strong. Then he lay down in a corner of his cage and shut his eyes. He did not like to look out through the bars at the jungle, when he could no longer roam about as he liked. Poor Nero was a prisoner—a caged wild animal.

For many days Nero was kept in the cage in the jungle near the hut of the black trapper. At first the lion would not eat, but at last he grew so hungry that he had to take some of the meat they thrust through the bars of the cage to him. And when he had eaten and taken some water, Nero felt better. But he was still cross and unhappy, and whenever any of the black Africans came near his cage Nero would suddenly stick out his paws and try to scratch them. But they knew enough to keep out of his way.

Then, one day, Nero felt his cage being suddenly lifted up on long poles, which the black men put across their shoulders, and so they carried the caged lion through the jungle. They wouldn't trust Nero to walk by himself. What had happened was that the white animal man, who bought wild animals for his circus, had come along, and, seeing that Nero was a fine lion, had taken him to be sent away across the ocean, from Africa to the United States of America, where there were many circuses.

Nero, still in his cage, was put on board a ship. He was stowed away down in a deep, black hole, deeper and blacker than the jungle pit into which he had fallen, and then began a sea voyage.

Nero didn't like this a bit. Sometimes he seemed to be standing on his head, and again he would be on his feet. At other times he seemed to roll over and over in a regular somersault. And these somersaults weren't at all like the ones he used to turn by accident, when he was playing tag in the jungle with his brother and sister, or with Switchie.

"Oh, dear, I don't like this at all!" grumbled Nero, in his cage in the ship. "I wish I could go back to the jungle. Oh, here I go again—upside down!"

And over he went, cage and all. What was happening was that the ship was in a big storm, and was being tossed up and down on great ocean waves, and that Nero's cage had got loose and was being flung about.

Our lion friend was seasick, and he had a dreadful time. More than once he wished himself back in the jungle, but he could not get there.

After many days the ship stopped tossing to and fro. It had crossed to the other side, with Nero on board, and was now tied up at a dock in New York. Then Nero felt himself being hoisted up in his cage, and, for the first time in many days, he saw the sun again and smelled fresh air. And, oh, how good it was!

It was not like the air of the jungle, for it was cooler, and Nero had been used to being very hot nearly all the time. But he did not mind being a bit cool.

Nero's cage was hoisted out of the hold, the deep, black hold of the ship, and slung on a big automobile truck with some boxes and barrels. Nero was the only wild animal, and people passing along on the dock stopped to look into the big wooden cage at the tawny yellow lion who had been brought all the way from the jungle.

Away started the auto-truck, giving Nero a new kind of ride. He would much rather have walked, but of course a lion can't go about loose in the streets of New York, though they do let the elephants and camels walk in a circus parade. But Nero was not yet in a circus.

Nero looked out through the bars of his cage as he was carted through the streets of New York.

"My, this is a queer jungle!" thought the lion. "Where are the trees and the tangled vines and the snakes and monkeys and other animals? All I see are men and other queer creatures. This isn't at all like my jungle!"

And of course it was not, being a big city. There are not many places for trees in a city, you know.

So Nero cowered down in the corner of his cage until he was put in a freight car to be sent to a place called Bridgeport, Connecticut, where some circus men keep their wild animals, to train them, and have them safe during the winter when it is too cold to give shows in the big, white tents.

"Well, this is a new sort of motion," thought Nero, as the train started off. "I don't know that I like it, but still it is better than being made to turn somersaults all the while."

Indeed it was easier riding on a train than in a ship; at least for Nero. He knew nothing about railroads, nor where he was being taken. But, after a while, during which he did not get much to eat or drink, once more his cage was put on a big auto-truck.

A little later, after being lifted about, and slung here and there, Nero suddenly saw one end of his cage open. The wooden bars, which had been around him ever since he had left the jungle, seemed to drop away.

"Ha! Now, maybe, I can get loose!" thought Nero.

He sprang forward, but, to his surprise, he found himself in very much the same sort of place. But this new cage was larger, and the bars were of iron instead of wood.

Looking through them Nero could see many other just such cages. He sniffed, and he smelled the smell of many wild animals which he knew. He smelled lions, buffaloes, and elephants.

Nero looked around him. He was in a big wooden building, and over to one side were some elephants. At first Nero could not believe it. He rubbed his eyes with his paw and looked again.

Yes, surely enough, they were elephants. They were swaying slowly to and fro, as elephants always sway, and they were stuffing hay into their mouths with their curling trunks.

"Oh, am I back in the jungle?" asked Nero aloud, speaking in animal talk.

"The jungle? No, I should say not!" cried a big jolly-looking elephant. "This isn't the jungle."

"Then what is it?" asked Nero.

"It's a circus," said the elephant. "This is a circus, and we are glad to have you with us, jungle lion. My name is Tum Tum, what is yours?"

"Nero," was the answer. "And so this is a circus!" went on the lion. "Well, well! I never thought I'd be here!"

CHAPTER VII

NERO LEARNS SOME TRICKS

Nero thought the circus a very queer place indeed. It was as queer to him as the wild jungle would be to you if you saw it for the first time. But strange as it was, the circus, where he now found himself, seemed much nicer to Nero than being cooped up in the dark ship or in the freight car.

For there were many wild animals in the circus—other lions, tigers, elephants, camels, giraffes, several cages of monkeys, some wolves, a bear or two, and others that Nero did not see until later. And there was also a queer, wild-animal smell, which Nero liked very much. It was almost like the smell of the jungle, and it made him homesick when he thought of the deep tangle of green vines, the thick trees and the silent pools of water.

"We are glad to have you in our circus," said the elephant, who had called himself Tum Tum, speaking to Nero. "Of course it isn't very lively now, but wait until we get out on the road, giving a show every day in a new place, and traveling about! Then you'll like it!"

"Doesn't the circus stay here every day?" asked Nero, as he looked across to another lion in a cage. Nero hoped this lion would speak to him, but the big fellow seemed to be asleep.

"The circus stay here? I should say not!" cried Tum Tum, speaking through his long trunk. "Why, this is only the winter barn, where we stay when the weather is cold. We don't have any shows in winter. The people don't come in to see us, and we don't do any of our tricks. It is only when the show goes on the road in summer, with the big white tent, all covered with gay flags, and the bands playing music, that we have the good times. Here we just rest, eat, and sometimes learn new tricks."

"Tricks!" exclaimed Nero. "Tricks? Are they something good to eat?"

"Tricks good to eat!" laughed Tum Tum in his jolly voice. "No indeed! Tricks are things you do. But often, after we do ours well, the trainer gives us good things to eat."

"I fell into a big hole in the jungle once," said Nero. "Is that a trick?"

"Not exactly," answered Tum Tum. "Here, I'll show you what a trick is. This is only one of my easy ones, though," and then suddenly the big elephant stood on his hind legs, waving his trunk in the air.

"Oh, so that's a trick," said Nero. "Well, I could do that."

But when he tried to stand up on his hind legs in his cage he could not. He had not learned how to balance himself.

"So you do tricks in a circus, do you?" went on Nero. "That reminds me. In the jungle I heard some monkeys speak of a circus, and also of a chap named Mappo. Is he here?"

"He used to be," said Tum Tum. "Mappo was one of our merriest monkeys. We all liked him, but he went to live with some people. I don't know where he is now. But he was in this circus. And to think of your meeting some of his friends in the jungle! Tell me, did you see any of mine?"

"Well, I met lots of elephants," answered Nero, "but I didn't have much time to stop and talk with them. I met a rhinoceros, though, and he said something about Chunky, a happy hippo, who used to live in the jungle near him."

"Oh, Chunky is here, in this very circus!" cried Tum Tum. "But he stays in a water-tank, so we don't very often see him. He'll be glad to know you met his rhinoceros friend. I'll tell him the first time I get a chance. But, speaking of tricks, there's a chap over there who does some fine ones," and Tum Tum pointed with his trunk to a cage in which was a shaggy, black animal.

"Who is it?" asked Nero.

"Dido, the dancing bear," answered the elephant. "He dances on a platform, which is strapped to my back out in the circus rings; he jumps through a hoop of blazing fire; and he turns somersaults."

"I turned some somersaults too, after they put me in a cage and brought me from the jungle," said Nero, as he thought of his voyage on the ship.

"Well, maybe you can learn to do them here, and that will be a trick," returned Tum Tum. "But you should see Dido, the dancing bear. He surely can dance!"

"Who is talking about me?" asked the shaggy creature in the other cage.

"We are, Dido," answered Tum Tum. "I was just telling the new lion how you dance on a platform over my back."

"Oh, yes," said the bear, opening wide his mouth and showing his red tongue. "And I wish I could soon start to doing that again. I am getting tired of the circus barn. I want to be out in the tent."

"It will soon be warm enough," said Tum Tum. "Summer will soon be here, and then we shall have hot weather."

"Does it get as hot as in the jungle?" Nero asked.

"Sometimes," answered the jolly elephant. "But here comes your keeper, I guess. He is going to give you some meat."

And, surely enough, along came a circus man with a big chunk of meat on a large, iron fork. He poked the meat in through the bars of the cage to Nero, and the lion was so hungry that he began eating at once.

The man who had fed him stood in front of the cage, looking at Nero.

"You look like a fine chap," said the man, talking partly to himself and partly to the jungle animal. "I think we shall be good friends, and I will teach you some tricks. Then the boys and girls who come to the circus will want to watch you. Yes, I'll teach you some tricks. Come, let's be friends."

Slowly and carefully the circus trainer reached his hand toward Nero's paw, which was between two bars and partly outside the cage. Nero, looking out of the corners of his eyes as he gnawed the bone and chewed the meat, did not know what the man was trying to do. Perhaps the lion thought that the man was trying to take away the meat.

Whatever he thought, Nero suddenly jumped up and struck with all his force at the man's hand. But the man was too quick. He pulled his hand out of the way, and Nero's paw hit the iron bars. And as it happened to be the paw that had been struck by the bullet, Nero felt great pain, for the bullet was still in the flesh, though healed over.

"Ouch!" cried Nero, in lion language.

"That will teach you not to strike at me when I am only trying to pat you and be kind to you," said the man with a laugh. "You are beginning to learn things, my lion friend."

The man stayed for some time in front of Nero's cage, talking kindly to the lion, but Nero paid no attention to him. He only ate the meat. Then, when it was all gone, Nero felt thirsty.

"I'll get you some water," said the man, and he did.

"Well, you are kind to me, anyhow," thought Nero, "even if you did try to take away my bone," but of course the man had not tried to do that.

For about a week Nero lived in his circus cage in the big barn, where the animals were kept warm all winter. Nothing much happened, except that the same man, every day, brought food and water to the wild jungle lion. And by this time Nero was not so wild as he had been at first. He gave up trying to break the iron bars with his paws, and no longer tried to bite them with his teeth. They were too strong for him.

Then, one day, the trainer man came again to the lion's cage, with a nice, sweet piece of meat.

"My, how good that is!" said Nero to himself, as he ate it.

As Nero was chewing away, the man slowly put out his hand toward the lion's paw, which was out between the bars. But Nero saw him, and again the old fear came back that the man was going to take away the meat, and Nero did not want that to happen.

"Look out!" roared Nero, in lion talk. "Look out or I'll scratch you!"

"Don't do that!" said another voice. A voice that Nero knew came from the other lion cage, that had recently been moved up near his. "Don't be silly, Nero!" said the other circus lion, whose name was Leo. "I used to be as wild as you are, and live in the jungle. But they caught me and brought me here to the circus; and now I like it very much. I, too, tried to scratch the man when he wanted to touch my paw, but I learned better. So must you. The man is your friend. He will feed you and give you water to drink. So don't scratch him. He only wants to pat you and rub you."

"Oh, well, if he only wants to do that, all right," said Nero. "He can do that. I thought he wanted to take my meat."

And then, when the man saw that Nero was quieting down, he reached out his hand again, and this time he touched Nero's big paw, with its sharp claws. One blow of it would have broken the man's arm, but Nero did not strike the blow. He had learned that the man would not hurt him.

And a few days after this Nero and the trainer had become such good friends that the man could open the iron door and go inside Nero's cage and the lion would only blink his big eyes, and not even growl. He had learned that the man would not hurt him.

And so Nero's circus lessons began. The first one he learned was leaping over a long stick which the man held stretched out in the cage. At the beginning Nero did not know what the stick was for, but he could see that the man did not intend to strike him with it.

The trainer kept bringing the stick nearer and nearer to Nero, who backed into the corner of the cage. At last the lion could back no farther, as he was close against the wall of the cage.

"Well, if he doesn't take that stick out of my way I'll jump right over it!" said Nero to himself. And that is just what he did, and the man clapped his hands in delight, and cried:

"There! You have learned your first trick! That's fine! Now I must teach you more!"

Nero was fast becoming a regular circus lion.

CHAPTER VIII

NERO MEETS DON

One day when Nero awoke in his circus cage, which stood in the big winter barn, the lion saw that something very different was going on from what had happened since he had been brought there from the jungle. Men were running to and fro, and the first thing Nero noticed was that Tum Tum, the jolly elephant, and all the other big animals with the long trunks were gone.

"Why, where is Tum Tum?" asked Nero of Leo, his lion friend.

"Oh, he's out with the other elephants, pushing wagon cages about the lot," said Leo.

"Pushing cages?" repeated Nero. "Is that a circus trick?"

"No, that is part of the circus work," answered Leo. "The elephants are so big and strong that they are used instead of horses, sometimes, to push the circus cages."

"But why is Tum Tum helping push the circus cages?" asked Nero. "Has anything happened?"

"Well, something is going to happen," said Leo. "The circus is going to start out on the road—we are going to travel from town to town. We are going to travel on the railroad and live in a tent instead of this barn. We shall see lots of people—boys and girls—who come to watch us eat, and do tricks, and we shall hear the band music and—Oh, it's real jolly!"

"I'm glad of that," said Nero. "I like to be jolly. But will Tum Tum come back?" he asked, for he liked the big, jolly elephant, as, indeed, all the circus animals did.

"Oh, yes, Tum Tum will come back," answered Dido, the dancing bear. "The circus couldn't get along without him. And I couldn't do some of my best tricks if Tum Tum didn't walk around the ring with the wooden platform on his back for me to dance on. Oh, we couldn't get along without Tum Tum!"

Nero was glad to hear this. Though he liked Leo, his lion friend, and the other animals, even the queer-looking camels, Nero felt more friendly toward Tum Tum than toward any one else in the circus except his trainer. For, by this time, Nero had grown to like very much the man who fed him, and who came into the cage every day to make the lion jump over the stick.

But Nero had learned many more tricks than this first, easy one. He did not learn the other tricks as quickly, for they were harder, but the lion could sit up on a big wooden stool, he could stand up on his hind paws, and he would open his mouth very wide when his trainer told him to. In a way Nero had learned something of man-talk, too, for he knew what certain words meant.

The trainer would call:

"Jump over the stick, Nero!"

The lion knew what that meant, and he knew it was different from the words used when the trainer said:

"Sit on your stool!"

So, though of course Nero could not understand what the circus men said when they talked to one another, the lion had learned some words. So he could talk and understand animal language, and he could also understand some words of man-talk. And that is pretty good, I think, for a lion who had not been out of the jungle quite a year.

"Shall we have to push any of the cages?" asked Nero of his friend Leo, as they both watched the circus men hurrying to and fro in the big barn.

"Oh, no," answered the older lion. "They never let us out of the cages."

"And a good reason, too," declared a humpy camel, near by. "If they let you lions and tigers out of the cages, you'd run away. We wouldn't do that. We camels are well-behaved, like the horses and the elephants."

Leo, the old lion, shook his head until his mane dangled in his eyes.

"No," he said, "if they opened my cage, I wouldn't run away. I wouldn't even go out, unless it was to get something to eat and come right back again."

"I would!" growled Nero. "I'd go out in a minute, if they opened my cage door wide enough. I'd go out and run back to the jungle."

"Yes, that's what I used to think, at first," growled Leo. "But after you've been in the circus awhile you get used to it. It's home to you.

"Why, I remember, Nero, we once had in this circus a lion just about like you. He always said he'd run away if he got the chance. Well, one day his cage was left open by accident, and he ran away."

"What happened?" asked Nero.

"Well, he ran back again, the next day, and a more sorry or sick-looking lion you never saw! He was bedraggled and lame and hungry and thirsty! He said he was glad to get back to his cage, and he never left it again."

"What had happened to him?" asked the camel. "I guess that was before my time."

"Oh, no sooner was he loose in the streets," said Leo, "than he was chased by men and boys, who threw rocks and sticks at him. They were afraid of him, and tried to drive him away. But the circus men tried to catch the runaway lion, and, between both, poor Tarsus, which was his name, had a bad time. He had enough of running away."

"He should have gone back to the jungle," said Nero. "That's what I'd do if I could get loose."

"Oh, you think you would!" growled Leo. "But the jungle is far away from here. You could never reach it. No, you had much better stay here in the circus, Nero. Here you are in a cage, it is true, but you are warm, you have a good place to sleep, you have plenty to eat and drink, and boys can not throw stones at you."

But Nero only switched his tail to and fro, thought of the jungle where he had played with Boo and Chet, and said to himself:

"That's all right. But, even though my trainer is kind to me, if ever I get the chance I'll run away!"

And so the circus got ready to go out on the road. Tum Tum and the other elephants pushed the animal cages about, and one day Nero saw the big elephant come close up to the lion's cage.

"What are you going to do, Tum Tum?" asked Nero.

"It is time for your cage to be moved," said the elephant. "I am going to push you out on the lot, and there horses will be hitched to your cage and you will be given a ride."

"Well, I hope the ride will be nice," said the lion.

"You'll like it," said Tum Tum, trumpeting through his trunk.

Pretty soon Nero found himself, in his cage, out in the bright sunshine. It was a warm day, and the lion stretched, opened his mouth as wide as he could, and then lay down in his cage where the sun could warm his back.

"It feels just as good as the jungle," thought Nero. "But of course there aren't as many trees, and there are no pools of water, and I haven't Switchie or Chet or Boo to play with. A circus may be nice, but I'll run away the first chance I get."

Tum Tum pushed Nero's cage about until some horses could be hitched to it to draw it to the railroad station. For the circus was to travel on a train of cars to the city where it was first to give a show.

Nero's cage, as well as other cages, were put on a big flat car, and when the engine started puffing and pulling away, and when Nero felt the motion of the train, he called to Leo, who was on the same car:

"I remember riding like this once before."

"Yes," said Leo, "I suppose so. It was when you were brought here from the big city where the ship landed. The same thing happened to me. But I am used to riding on railroads now. I don't mind it any more. I like it."

"I guess I'll like it, too," said Nero.

For the rest of that day and all the night the circus train traveled onward, and it was nearly morning when it stopped. Peeping out between the cracks of the wooden cover of his cage, Nero could see the sun just coming up. It reminded him of the sunrise in the jungle, and he began to feel lonesome and homesick again, even though he had new friends — Tum Tum, Dido and Leo.

There was a great deal of noise when the circus train stopped. Men shouted, horses kicked about in their wooden cars, the elephants trumpeted, the tigers growled, the lions roared, while the monkeys chattered.

Nero felt his cage being run down off the car, and then he heard Tum Tum talking in elephant animal language.

"How are you, Nero? All right?" asked Tum Tum, as he pushed the lion's cage about so the horses could be hitched to it again. "Are you ready to do your tricks in the circus?"

"Oh, yes," answered Nero. "When do we begin?"

"Pretty soon," answered Leo from his cage. "We'll go to the circus lot, then will come the parade, and then we'll be put in the big tent for the boys and girls to look at. Then the bands will play and the performance will start."

"My! that's a lot of things to happen," said Nero.

Pretty soon one side of his cage was opened, and Nero's trainer passed by.

"Hello, Nero, old boy!" called the man. "Did you stand the ride all right? Yes, I guess you did. Well, we'll soon be doing our tricks together in the tent," and he patted the paw Nero held out to him, for this was his way of shaking hands.

Soon after this Nero felt his cage being hauled along by a team of eight horses. The wooden outside covers of the cage were still down, and Nero could look out through the bars, and the people could look in. Then Nero saw that many of the other cages of wild animals were in line with his, some in front and some behind. There were many horses, elephants and camels in line also, and a band was playing music.

"What's all this about?" asked Nero of Tum Tum.

"We are going in the circus parade, through the streets of the town," answered the jolly elephant. "We always have a parade before the show. You'll like it."

And Nero liked, very much indeed, his first parade. His keeper rode in the cage with him, sitting on a chair, and now and then patting the big head of the lion. Nero liked that, for he and his keeper were friends. Through great crowds of people on the streets went the circus parade, and then the procession went back to the circus lot where the big, white tents, with their gaily colored flags, had been set up.

"Pretty soon the show will begin, Nero," said the keeper, as he got out of the lion's cage. "The parade was only the first part. The people will shortly be in here to look at you and the other animals, and, later on, you and I will do some tricks."

All at once, as the trainer walked away, Nero looked out of his cage and saw a big shaggy animal running along on the ground.

"Hello, Dido!" growled Nero, for at first he thought it was the dancing bear he saw. But as the running animal turned, Nero saw that it was not Dido. This animal was not so large as the dancing bear.

"I'm not Dido," said the new chap. "And I don't seem to know you, though I know that bear in the cage back of you."

"Why, that's who I thought you were," said Nero. "And so you know Dido?"

"Oh, yes, I know him, and Dido knows me," said the new animal.

"Well, you'd better go back into your cage before the circus men see you," said Nero. "How did you get loose? Tell me? I'd like to get out myself."

"Ho! Ho! You're making a mistake!" was the laughing answer. "I am not a circus animal. I'm Don, and I'm a runaway dog. At least I ran away once, but I ran back again. I came down to see Dido, whom I met when I was running away," and Don, the nice, big dog, wagged his tail at Dido, the dancing bear.

CHAPTER IX

NERO SCARES A BOY

Nero, the circus lion, who was much larger now than when he had been caught in a jungle trap, was very much surprised at what Don, the runaway dog told him. At first the lion boy could hardly believe that Don was not one of the circus animals.

But as the lion, looking out through the bars of his cage, saw Don running about and none of the red-coated circus men trying to catch him, he said:

"Well, well! it must be true. He isn't a circus animal at all." And then to Don the lion said:

"How do you happen to know Dido, the dancing bear?"

"Well, that's a long story," answered Don. "You can read all about me, and how I ran away, if you want to, for it's all in a book a man wrote about me."

"Thank you," returned Nero. "But I can't read, and I don't know what a book is, anyhow."

"Well, I can't read, either," said Don. "But I know a book when I see one. The little boy in the house where I live goes to school, and he has books. Sometimes I carry them home for him in my mouth. So I know a book when I see one.

"But as long as you can't read about me I'll just tell you that in the book the man wrote about how I ran away, got locked in a freight car, how I went to a strange city and traveled about the country. It was then I met Dido, the dancing bear."

"Yes, that's right," growled Dido, licking his paws, for some one had thrown him a sugared popcorn ball, and some of the sweet, sticky stuff was still on the bear's paws. Dido wanted to get all of it off. "It was then you met me, Don," went on the dancing bear. "We certainly had some fine times together!"

"Indeed we did!" replied the runaway dog, though I should not call him that any more, as he had run back again, as you all know, and was now living in a nice home. "And when I was down at the butcher shop this morning and saw the circus wagons come from the railroad yard," went on Don, "I thought maybe I'd see you again, Dido. So I came here as soon as I could."

"I'm glad you did," said the bear. "This lion chap is named Nero. He hasn't been out of the jungle very long."

"I'm glad to meet you, Nero," barked Don. "I always like circus animals."

"I am glad you do," growled Nero, in his most jolly voice. "I think I shall like you, too, Don, though I don't know much about dogs. I never saw any in the jungle."

And this was true, for though there are some dogs in Africa, they are mostly in cities or the towns where the native black men live. There may be some wild dogs in the jungle, but Nero never saw any, and the nearest he ever came to noticing animals like a dog were the black-backed jackals. These are animals, almost like a dog, and, in fact, are something like the Azara dogs of South America, and now Nero asked Don if he was a jackal.

But the runaway dog soon told the circus lion a different story, and then they were friends. Don and Dido had a nice visit together in the circus tent before the show began. Don had simply slipped under the side of the tent to get in. If any of the circus men saw him they did not mind, for dogs often come around where circus shows are given. Perhaps they like to see the elephants and other strange animals, as much as the boys and girls do.

After awhile great crowds of people began coming into the circus tent. The band played music in another tent, next door, and it was there that the men and women performers would do their tricks—riding on the backs of galloping horses, leaping about on trapezes, jumping over the backs of elephants and so on.

Nero paced back and forth in his cage, wondering what was going to happen, for this was his first day of real life in the circus. All the other days had been just getting ready for the summer shows.

He had liked the parade through the city streets, when the elephants, horses, and camels wore such bright and gaily colored blankets. Now something else was going to happen.

The animal tent, in which stood Nero's cage and that of the other jungle folk, was soon filled with boys and girls and their fathers and mothers, all of whom had come to the circus. They moved from cage to cage, stopping to toss popcorn balls to Dido, the dancing bear, and feed peanuts to Tum Tum, the jolly elephant, and to the friends of Mappo and some of the other merry monkeys.

Coming to the cage of the big lion, the boys and girls would stop and look in, and perhaps some one would say:

"Oh, isn't he big and fierce! I wouldn't want to go into his cage!"

And perhaps some one else would answer:

"Pooh! I guess he's a trained lion! Maybe he does tricks! When I grow up I'm going to be a lion tamer."

Of course Nero did not understand any of this talk, but he liked to look at the boys and girls, and he was not nearly as wild as he had been when he lived in the jungle. Nero was really quite tame, and he liked his trainer very much, for the man was kind to Nero.

Pretty soon all the people—even the boys and girls—went out of the animal tent, leaving the animals almost alone.

"Where have they gone?" asked Nero of Dido.

"Oh, into the other tent, where the music is playing and where the performance is going on. You'll soon be going in there too, and so shall I."

"What for?" asked Nero.

"To do your tricks," answered the bear. "That is why you were taught to do them, just as I was taught to dance—so we can make fun and jolly times for the boys and girls. Wait, and you'll see."

And, surely enough, a little later Nero's cage was moved into the larger tent, next to the one where the animals were kept. And then Nero's trainer came and spoke to him.

"Well, Nero," said the man, "now we're going to see if you can do your tricks before a whole crowd, as nicely as you did them in the barn at Bridgeport. Don't grow excited. You know I'm a friend of yours. Now do your best, and the boys and girls will laugh and clap their hands."

So the keeper opened the door of the lion's cage and went inside. As soon as he did several of the boys and girls, and the big folks too, gasped, and some said:

"Oh, isn't that terrible! I wouldn't go into the cage of a real, live lion for anything!"

You see they didn't know Nero was quite tame, and that the jungle beast liked the man who fed him and was kind to him.

"Now do your tricks, Nero!" said the trainer.

And Nero did. He jumped over a stick; he stood up on his hind legs and, putting his paws on the trainer's shoulders, made believe to kiss the man, though of course he only touched the man's cheek with his cold, damp nose, just as, sometimes, your dog puts his nose against your cheek to show how much he likes you; next Nero stood up on a sort of upside-down washtub, or pedestal; and after that he jumped through a hoop covered with paper.

"And now, ladies and gentlemen," said the trainer, speaking to the circus crowd, "I will do the best trick of all. I will have Nero, my pet lion, open his mouth as wide as he can, and I will put my head inside!"

And then, all of a sudden, some little boy in the crowd piped up and cried out:

"Oh, Mister, don't do that! He might bite your head off!"

Everybody laughed at that, even Nero's trainer, who said:

"Oh, I'm not afraid. Nero is a good lion and wouldn't bite me. Come on now, old fellow, for the last and best trick of all!" cried the man, and he cracked his whip, though of course he did not strike Nero with it.

The circus lion knew just what to do, for he had been trained in this trick. I didn't say anything about it before, because I was saving it as a surprise for you.

"Open your mouth!" suddenly cried the trainer, and Nero opened his jaws as wide as he could.

"Oh! Ah! Look!" cried the people, as they saw his big, red tongue and the white, sharp teeth.

"Now!" cried the trainer, and into the lion's mouth he popped his head.

Everybody in the big circus tent was quiet for a moment, and then all the crowd cried out, and clapped their hands and stamped their shoes on the wooden steps beneath their feet.

"There, you see how tame my lion is!" cried the man, as he pulled his head from Nero's mouth, and bowed to the people, who were still clapping and whistling.

"You are a good lion!" said the trainer to Nero in a low voice. "Now you shall have a nice piece of meat, a sweet bone to gnaw, and a good drink of water. You did your first tricks very well indeed."

Nero did not quite know what it was all about, but he felt that he had done well. It did not hurt him to open his mouth and let the man put in his head, but it tickled the lion's tongue a little, so that Nero wanted to sneeze. And that wouldn't have been a good thing for the trainer. However Nero didn't do it.

"What makes the people make so much noise?" asked Nero of Dido, the dancing bear, who came into the larger tent just then.

"Oh, that's because they liked your tricks," was the answer. "They always clap and stamp their feet when anything pleases them. They do that when I dance on the platform on Tum Tum's back."

And, surely enough, the circus crowds did. They liked the tricks of Dido, the dancing bear, as much as they had those of Nero.

After a while Nero's cage was wheeled back into the tent where the wagons of the other animals were kept, and Nero was given something good to eat, and fresh water to drink. Then he felt happy and fell asleep.

So Nero began his circus life, and he kept it up all that summer. He traveled about from place to place, and soon became used to doing his tricks, having the man put his head into his mouth and seeing the crowds show their surprise.

One day, when the show was being given in a large city, there was a big crowd in the animal tent. Near Nero's cage were some boys, and I am sorry to say they were not all kind boys, though perhaps they didn't know any better. One of the boys had a rotten apple in his hand and he said to another lad:

"I'm going to give this rotten apple to one of the elephants and see what a funny face he makes when he chews it!"

"That'll be lots of fun," said the second boy.

I don't, myself, call that fun. It isn't fair to fool animals when you know so much more than they do. However we'll see what happened.

Nero saw the boys standing near his cage, and he heard them talking, though he did not, of course, know what they were saying. But he could smell the rotten apple. Often, in the jungle, he had smelled bad fruit, and he knew that the monkeys would not eat it.

"If bad fruit isn't good for monkeys it isn't good for elephants," thought Nero, as he saw the boy hold out the rotten apple toward Tum Tum, the jolly elephant.

Tum Tum reached out his trunk to take what he thought was something good, but Nero roared, in animal language, of course:

"Don't take that apple, Tum Tum! It's bad!" And then Nero sprang against the bars of his cage, and, reaching out a paw, with its long, sharp claws, made a grab for the boy's arm as he held out the rotten apple.

"Look out! The lion's going to bite you!" cried a man to the boy, and the boy was so frightened that he gave a howl and dropped the rotten apple and ran through the crowd, knocking to the right and left every one in his way.

Nero roared again and dashed against the bars of his cage, and while women and children screamed and men shouted, Nero's keeper and some of the other animal men ran up to see what the matter was. There was great excitement in the circus tent.

CHAPTER X

NERO RUNS AWAY

Once more Nero roared as he looked over the heads of the crowd to see what had become of the boy who had tried to give Tum Tum the rotten apple.

"Hold on there, my lion boy! What's the matter? Don't do that!" called Nero's trainer to him in a kind voice. "What happened, anyhow? Why are you roaring so, and trying to get out of your cage? Don't you like it here in the circus?"

Nero stopped roaring at once, and no longer dashed against the bars of his cage. Perhaps he thought that, as long as his kind trainer was at hand, everything would be all right.

"Did some one try to hurt my lion friend?" asked the trainer, looking at the crowd near the cage.

"No," some one answered. "But the lion, all at once, tried to reach out and claw a boy who was going to give an apple to an elephant. I saw that. I don't know what made the lion act so."

"There must have been some good reason," said the trainer. "Nero is a good lion. He wouldn't want to claw a boy just for fun."

And then one of the other boys, who was in the crowd that had been around the lad who had the rotten apple, spoke up and said:

"Mister, Jimmie was going to play a trick on the elephant. He was going to give him a bad apple just to see what a funny face the elephant would make."

"Oh, ho! Now I understand!" said the trainer. "My lion must have smelled the rotten apple and didn't like it. He tried to scare away the boy, I guess."

"Well, the boy was scared all right," said a man. "He ran away as fast as he could go."

"He ought to!" said the trainer very sharply.

The excitement, caused by the loud roaring of Nero, was over now, though, for a time, many persons had been frightened, for Nero had sent his powerful voice rumbling through the circus tent as his father, and the other big lions, had used to make the ground tremble when they roared in the jungle.

Then, as things grew quiet and the people passed along the row of cages, looking at the animals, Tum Tum, who heard what had happened, turned to Nero and said:

"I'm much obliged to you, my dear lion friend, for scaring the boy who wanted to give me the rotten apple. Most likely, as soon as I'd have taken it in my trunk, I'd have smelled that it was bad, and I would not have eaten it. But some one might have given me a popcorn ball in my trunk at the same time, and that might have smelled so good that I wouldn't have noticed the rotten apple until too late. So you saved me from having a bad taste in my mouth, and I'm much obliged to you."

"Oh, that's all right," replied Nero. "I'm glad I could do you a favor. You have been kind to me, pushing my cage around, and I want to be kind to you."

So the two circus animals were better friends than ever, and that day in the performers' tent Nero opened his mouth very wide indeed when his trainer wanted to put in his head.

For many weeks Nero traveled about the country with the circus, living in his iron-barred cage, from which he was never taken. Nero might be a tame lion, but the circus folk did not think it would be safe to let him out, as Dido, the dancing bear, was allowed to come out of his cage.

However, later on, something happened—

But there, I must tell about it in the right place.

So, as I said, Nero went about from town to town with the circus, living in his cage, eating and doing his tricks whenever his trainer called on him to do so. And the people who came to the circus performances seemed to like, very much, seeing Nero do his tricks. And they always clapped loudest and longest when the trainer put his head in the lion's mouth. And Nero never bit the trainer once, nor so much as scratched him, even with the tip of one sharp tooth.

One afternoon of a long hot day, when big crowds had come to the circus, and after Nero had done his tricks, and Dido, the dancing bear, had done his, and Chunky, the happy hippo, had opened his big mouth so his keeper could toss loaves of bread into it—one afternoon Tum Tum, the jolly elephant, swaying as he chewed his hay, spoke through his trunk and said:

"Something is going to happen!"

"What makes you think so?" asked Nero, from his cage.

"Well, I sort of feel it," answered Tum Tum. "I think we are going to have a big thunderstorm, such as we used to have in the jungle!"

"I hope we do!" growled a striped tiger in a cage next to Nero. "I like a good thunder storm, where the rain comes down and cools you off! I like to feel the squidgie mud of the jungle, too, and when it thunders I growl as loudly as I can. I like a storm. I want to get wet!"

"I like a thunder storm, too," said Tum Tum. "But you animals in your cages—you lions and tigers—aren't very likely to feel any rain. We elephants will get wet, and so will the camels and the horses, for we walk out in the open. But, Nero, I guess you in your cage won't feel the storm any."

"No, I don't believe we shall," agreed the lion. "But I wish we could. I am so hot and dry, sitting in this cage, that I wish I could get out and splash around in the mud and water. So the sooner the thunder storm comes the better."

"It isn't likely to do you much good," went on Tum Tum, "but it will be cooler, afterward, anyhow."

And it certainly was very hot in the circus tent that day. It did not get much cooler after dark, and when the circus was over, and the big tents taken down, it was still hot.

"We are not going to travel on the train to go to the next town where the circus is to show," said Tum Tum to Nero, as the men began hitching horses to the animal cages and the big tent wagons. "We are to go along the road, in the open."

"Then maybe I can see the lightning!" exclaimed Nero. "And, if it rains, I can stick my paws out through the bars and get them wet."

"Maybe," said Tum Tum. Then he had to go off to help push some of the heavy wagons, and it was some time before Nero saw his big elephant friend again.

Soon the circus caravan was traveling along the road in the darkness. And yet it was not dark all the time, for, every now and then, there came a flash of lightning. The thunder rumbled, too, like the distant roaring of a band of lions.

"The storm will soon be here," said the striped tiger, as he crouched down in one corner of his cage, which, like that of Nero, was being hauled along the road by eight horses.

"Well, we'll feel better when it rains," said the lion.

And then, all at once, the wind began to blow, there came a brighter flash of lightning, a loud clap of thunder, and the storm broke. Down came the rain, in "buckets full," as is sometimes said, and the horses, camels and elephants loved to feel the warm water splashing down on their backs, cooling them off and washing away the dust and dirt.

Some of the rain even dashed into the cages of Nero and the tiger, and the jungle cats liked the feel of it as much as did the other circus beasts.

But the rain did something else, too. It made the roads very soft and slippery with mud, and in the middle of the night, when Nero's cage was being pulled up a steep hill, something broke on the wagon. It got away from the horses and began to roll down the hill backward.

"Look out! Look out!" cried the driver, as he tried to put on the brake. "The lion's cage is running away downhill! Look out, everybody! Look out behind there, Bill on the tiger's cage! Look out!"

But the lion's cage did not crash into the tiger's cage, which was the next wagon behind. Instead, Nero's house on wheels rolled to one side of the road and toppled over into a ditch. There was a loud crash as the wooden sides and top cracked and broke.

All at once Nero saw the door of his broken cage swing open. He could walk right out, and, as soon as he got steady on his feet, after being tossed about by the fall, the lion gave a leap and found himself standing clear of his cage in the soft mud, with the rain beating down all about him.

"Why—why, I'm loose!" roared Nero. "I'm out of my cage for the first time since I was caught in the jungle! Oh, and this is like the jungle, a little. I can feel the soft mud on my paws, and the rain on my back!"

Nero opened his mouth to roar, and the rain dashed in, cooling his tongue. As the lightning flashed he could see his broken cage at one side of the ditch, but he was clear of it. When the thunder roared Nero roared back in answer.

Up above him Nero could hear the circus men shouting. What they were saying he did not know, but they were telling one another that the lion's cage had rolled downhill, had broken, and that the lion was loose.

Nero looked around him. He could see quite well in the dark. Off to one side he saw some tangled bushes and a clump of trees.

"Maybe that is the jungle!" thought Nero. "I'm going to find out. I'm going to leave the circus for a while. It was very nice, but I want to be free. I want to feel the rain and the mud. Now that I am out of my cage I'll stay loose for a time!"

And so Nero ran away!

CHAPTER XI

NERO AND BLACKIE

The first thing any wild animal does when it runs away is to find some dark place and hide. Even though it may be hungry, an animal, when frightened, will nearly always hide until it can look about and make up its mind what to do.

Nero, the circus lion, who got loose from his cage when it rolled downhill in the storm and broke open, did this thing. When he had stood for a moment in the rain and darkness, feeling the soft mud squdge up between his claws, and when he had roared a bit, because he felt so wild and free, Nero sneaked off in the darkness toward some trees and bushes, which he had seen in a flash of lightning.

"That may be the jungle," he had said to himself.

But of course you and I know that it wasn't the jungle. That was far, far away — across the sea in Africa.

He stood for a moment, listening to the shouts of the circus men, who were standing about the broken cage. They could not see Nero in the darkness, nor even when the lightning flashed, for the lion crouched down behind some black bushes.

"Well, Nero got away all right," said one circus man.

"Yes, and we must get him back!" said the man who had trained Nero to do his tricks. "Folks don't like lions wandering about their farms and gardens. I must find my pet. Here, Nero! Nero! Come back!" called the trainer.

But though the lion liked the man who had been so kind to him, Nero was not yet ready to go back to the circus.

"I have just gotten out of my cage," said Nero to himself; "and it would be too bad to go back before I have had some fun. So I'll just run on and stay in the jungle awhile."

Nero felt very happy. It was a long time since he had been able to roam about as he pleased, and though he had no raincoat or umbrella, and not even rubbers, he didn't mind the storm at all. Animals like to get wet, sometimes, if the rain is not too cold. It gives them a bath, just as you have yours in a tub.

"This certainly is fun!" said Nero to himself, as he trotted along through the rain and darkness toward the trees. "I'll find a good place to hide in and stay there all night."

It did not take Nero long to find a hiding place. It was a sort of cave down in between two big rocks in the woods; and it was almost as good as the cave in which he had lived in the jungle with his father and mother and Chet and Boo.

"I wish my brother and sister were here now," thought Nero to himself, as he snuggled down on a bed of dry leaves between the rocks. The leaves were dry because one rock stretched over them, like a roof. "And if Switchie were here he and I could have some fun to-morrow, going about this new jungle," thought the lion boy.

But Switchie, the lion cub with whom Nero used to play, was far off in Africa, so our circus friend had to stay by himself. He curled up on the leaves, listened to the swish and patter of the rain, and soon he fell asleep.

Now while Nero was hiding thus in the cave he had found, the circus men were anxious to find the lion. They got ropes and lanterns, and had a new, empty cage made ready, so that, in case Nero were found, he could be given a new home. Then, while Nero's trainer and some men to help him hunt for the lion stayed behind, the rest of the circus went on to where it was to give a show the next day. No matter what happens, the circus must go on, if there is any of it left to travel. Accidents often happened like this one—cages getting stuck in the mud and animals sometimes getting away.

But I'm not going to tell you, just now, about the circus men who stayed behind to hunt Nero. They did not find the lion very easily. This story is mostly about Nero, so we shall now see what happened to him.

All night long Nero slept in the cave. It lightened and thundered, but he did not mind that. Nor did he mind the rain, for though he had been wet, he liked it, and in the cave under the rock no more water could splash on him.

When Nero awoke the sun was shining through the leaves and branches of the trees and down in through the tangle of bushes in front of the cave where Nero had hidden. The lion rolled over, stretched out his heavy paws with their big, curved claws, and opened his mouth and yawned, just as you have often seen your dog or cat yawn after a sleep.

"Well," said Nero to himself, "I guess I'll look around this jungle and see if I can find any breakfast. I'm hungry, and that nice trainer man isn't here to give me anything to eat. I'll have to hunt for it myself, as I used to do when I was at home. We'll see what kind of jungle this is."

Nero soon found that it was quite different from the jungle in Africa. The trees were not so big, nor were there so many of them, and the vines and bushes were not so tangled. It was not quite so hot, either, though this was the middle of summer, and there were not as many birds as Nero was used to seeing in his home jungle. Nor were there any monkeys swinging by their tails from the trees. It was quite a different jungle altogether, but Nero liked it better than his circus cage.

"Now for something to eat!" said Nero, when he had finished stretching. He stepped from the little cave out into the bright sunshine, and looked around. He wanted to make sure there were no men near by who might catch him and take him back to that queer house on wheels, with iron bars all around it. Nero saw nothing to make him go back into his cave.

Up in the trees the robins and the sparrows sang and chirped, but if they saw the tawny, yellow lion moving about, like a big cat, they paid no attention. They did not seem to mind Nero at all.

And, pretty soon, Nero found something to eat in the woods. He had not forgotten how to hunt, as he had done in the jungle, though it was rather a long time ago.

Then Nero sniffed and sniffed until he found a spring of water, at which he took a good drink.

"Well, now that I have had something to eat and something to drink I feel much better," said Nero to himself. "I must have some fun."

So he looked about, wondering what he would do. It was a sort of vacation for him, you see, as he did not have to do any of his circus tricks.

"Let's see, now," thought Nero. "I wonder —"

And then, all of a sudden, the lion heard a rustling noise over in the bushes at one side. He gave a jump, just as your cat does when something startles her. Nero wanted to be on the watch for any one who might be trying to catch him or trap him.

Then Nero saw a small black animal walk slowly out from under a big bush. The animal was something like a little tiger, except that she was plain black instead of being striped yellow and black. At first Nero was much surprised.

"Hello, there!" called the lion, in animal talk, which is the same all over the world. "Hello there! Who are you and where are you going?"

"Oh, I'm Blackie, a cat," was the answer. "Once I was a lost cat, but I'm not that way any longer. Who are you, if I may ask?"

CHAPTER XII

NERO AND THE TRAMP

Nero, the circus lion, gave himself a big shake. His mane, or big fringe of hair around his neck, stood out like the fur on your cat's back when a dog chases her, and then Nero roared. Oh, such a loud roar as he gave! The ground shook.

"There! Now do you know who I am?" asked Nero.

Blackie, the cat who was once lost, seemed quite surprised at the way Nero acted. She looked at the lion and said:

"Well, I'm sure I don't know why in the world you are making so much noise. I just asked what your name was, and there you go acting as though you were a part of a thunderstorm. What's it all about, anyhow?"

"I was just telling you my name," said Nero, a little ashamed of himself for having made such a racket. "I'm a circus lion. At least I used to be in a circus, but I ran away last night, when my cage rolled downhill and broke."

"Oh, a circus lion!" mewed Blackie. "Why, I know some folks in a circus. There was Dido, a dancing bear, and—"

"Why, I know him too!" roared Nero, in delight. "He's in the same circus I came from!"

"You don't tell me!" exclaimed Blackie. "And then I knew Tum Tum, a jolly elephant, and—"

"Well, say now, isn't that queer?" laughed Nero—at least he laughed as much as a lion ever laughs. "Why, Tum Tum is in my circus, too! We are great friends. And once a dog named Don came to the show, but he did not stay very long."

"Oh, I know Don, too," said Blackie. "Once he ran away, and once he chased me. But that was before we were friends. Say, Nero, I feel as if I had known you a long time, since we know so many of the same friends. Tell me, have you ever been in a book?"

"There it goes again!" cried Nero. "Book! Book! Book! Tum Tum is in one, and so is Don, and Dido. I suppose, next, you'll be telling me that you have had a book written about you."

"Yes," said Blackie, rather slowly, as she waved her tail to and fro, "a man wrote a book about me. It tells how I got lost, how I was in a basket, and how I came home to find the family all away. And maybe I wasn't glad when they came back! But were you ever in a book?"

"No," answered the circus lion, "and I never expect to be."

But that only goes to show that Nero didn't know anything about it. For he is in a book, isn't he?

"Where do you live?" asked Nero of Blackie. "Is it in a circus?"

"Gracious sakes alive, no!" exclaimed Blackie. "I wouldn't know what to do in a circus. I live in that house over there with a little boy and girl who are very kind to me. Wouldn't you like to come over and see them?"

"Thank you, no. Not just now," Nero answered. "I'm not much used to being around houses, though I like boys and girls, for I see many of them in the circus, and they like to watch me do my tricks. But I have just run away, and I want to go about by myself a bit more. The men from the circus may try to catch me, you know."

"Don't you want them to?" asked Blackie.

"Well, not right away," answered the lion. "I want to have some fun by myself first."

"Well, I must be going," said Blackie after a bit, when she had talked a little further with Nero. "If ever you're around my house, stop in and see me. It's right over there, across the hill," and she pointed to it with her paw.

"I will, thank you," said Nero, switching his tail from side to side. Then Blackie said goodbye to him, and the cat walked on through the woods, back toward the house where she lived.

For two or three days Nero wandered about in the woods, and, all this while, the circus men were hunting everywhere for him. But they could not find him, for the lion kept well hidden in the woods. And of course, though Blackie knew he was there, she could not speak man-talk to tell about him. So Nero remained free and had a good time.

But one day the circus lion felt lonesome. He had met none of his friends in the woods, and had not seen Blackie again, though he had looked for her. Nero did meet a little animal who seemed quite friendly. This was Slicko, the jumping squirrel, and Slicko had a nice talk with the lion.

"I know what I'll do," said Nero to himself one day. "I'll go over to that house where Blackie lives and see her."

So Nero started over the hill to go to the house that Blackie had pointed out as the one in which she lived. And a very strange thing happened to the circus lion there.

As it happened, when Nero slunk out of the woods, which were near Blackie's house, no one saw him. In fact none of the family was at home, having gone visiting for the day. Blackie wasn't at home, either, having gone down in the cow pasture to hunt grasshoppers, so there was no one in the house. But Nero did not know that. He went sniffing and snuffing around, thinking perhaps he could find something to eat, but nothing had been left out for lions, as Blackie's folks did not know one was roaming about so near them.

Nero walked softly up to the kitchen door of the house. The door was partly open, and this was strange, if the lion had only known it, for folks don't usually go away and leave doors open behind them. And from the open door came the smell of something good. It was the smell of meat, and, in fact, was a boiled ham, which Blackie's mistress had left in a pot on the stove.

Now the reason the door of the farmhouse was open was because it had been broken open by a tramp! This tramp, coming to the house to ask for something to eat and seeing that no one was at home, had broken open the door. He was going to get something to eat, and then take whatever else he wanted. And that's why the door was open when Nero walked up to it. The tramp was in the kitchen, cutting himself some pieces from the cold, boiled ham.

"My, that smells good!" thought Nero, as he sniffed the meat. "I guess I'll go in and see if I can't get some."

So Nero, not, of course, knowing anything about the tramp, but wanting only to get some meat and, perhaps, see his friend Blackie, pushed the kitchen door open with his nose and walked in.

And then, all of a sudden, that bad, ragged tramp, who had come in to steal, looked up from the table where he was sitting, eating ham, and saw the lion.

"Oh, my! Oh, my goodness me!" cried the tramp, and he was so surprised and frightened that he just slumped down in his chair and didn't dare move. The piece of meat he had been eating dropped from his hand to the floor, and Nero picked it up and ate it, licking his jaws for more.

"Oh, this is terrible!" gasped the tramp. "I didn't know this farmer kept a trained lion as a watchdog. I knew he had a black cat, but not a lion. Oh, what am I to do?"

Of course Nero didn't in the least know what the man was talking about. But the lion smelled the meat and he wanted some more; so he sat down in front of the kitchen door and looked at the ragged man.

"I don't know who you are," said Nero to himself, "and you are certainly not as nice as my circus trainer.

"But you have some more meat there," Nero thought on, for he could still smell the ham on the table. "I think you might give me a bit more. That little piece was hardly enough."

And so Nero sat there looking at the tramp, who was too frightened to move. He couldn't get out of the door, because the lion was in the way, and he didn't dare turn his back, to go over to open a window and jump out, for fear the lion would spring on him.

"Oh, I'm in a terrible fix!" thought the tramp. "This is the first time I was ever caught by a lion! It's worse than half a dozen dogs! Oh, what shall I do?"

There really did not seem to be anything for him to do except just sit there. And Nero sat looking at him, waiting to be fed some more meat, as he had been used to being fed in the circus.

And then something else happened. Back to the house came the farmer and his wife, and their little girl was with them. They had returned from their visit.

"Why, look, Mother!" cried the little girl, as she went up on the back porch. "The kitchen door is open!"

"It is?" cried her mother. "I'm sure we locked it when we went away."

"We did," said the farmer, who was the little girl's father. "Some one must have gone in—a tramp, maybe. I'll see about this!"

The farmer walked quickly to the kitchen door and opened it wide. It had swung partly shut after Nero had gone in. And when the farmer saw the frightened tramp sitting in the chair at the table, too scared to move, and the lion between him and the door, on guard, it seemed, the farmer was so surprised and frightened himself that he cried:

"Oh my! There's a lion in our kitchen, and a tramp! Oh, I must get my gun! I must send for the constable!"

"The constable won't be any good for a lion," said the farmer's wife.

"No, but my gun can shoot the lion," said the farmer. "I'll go for it."

"Oh, let me see the lion!" begged the little girl. "I saw one in the circus the other day, and he was tame. Maybe this is the same one. The circus lion I saw wouldn't bite any one, even when the man put his head in the big mouth. Let me look!"

She pushed past her father and mother, and looked in the kitchen. The little girl saw the frightened tramp, who had been caught by the lion, and the little girl also saw Nero. And then she laughed and shouted:

"Why, that's the very same nice, tame lion I saw in the circus! I'm sure it's the very same one, for it looks just like him. But I can soon tell."

"Gracious goodness, child!" cried her mother. "Don't dare go near him! Besides, it may not be a tame, circus lion."

"Well, if he is he can do tricks," said the little girl. "The lion I saw in the circus sat up on a stool when the trainer told him to. We haven't any stool big enough, but maybe I can make the lion sit on his hind legs on the table. That will hold him."

And then the little girl, doing just as she had seen the trainer do in the circus, held up her hand, pointed at the lion in the kitchen, and then at the table, and cried:

"Up, Nero! Up! Sit on the table!"

And though Nero did not know the little girl, and did not remember having seen her before, the trained lion knew what the words meant. He had heard his trainer say them many, many times. So Nero slowly walked over to the table, got up on it with a jump, and then and there, right in front of the tramp and the little girl and her father and mother, Nero sat on his hind legs on the table, just as he was accustomed to sit on a stool in the circus ring.

"There! What did I tell you?" cried the little girl, clapping her hands. "I knew he was the tame, circus lion! Doesn't he sit up nice?"

"Yes," said the farmer, "he does. But there is no telling how long he may sit there. He must have escaped from the circus, and I had better telephone the men that he is here. They'll be glad to get him back."

"It's a good thing he scared the tramp," said the farmer's wife, as she looked at the ragged man. "What are you doing here, anyhow?" she asked him.

"I—I just came in to get something to eat," he whined. "And then your lion wouldn't let me go."

"He isn't my lion," replied the farmer. "But he's done me a good turn. I'll have the constable come here and take you away."

And a little later the constable, who had been telephoned for, came and took the tramp to jail. Nero looked on, wondering what it was all about, and wishing some one would give him something to eat. And the little girl thought of this.

"The tramp has spoiled the ham for us, Mother," she said. "Can't I give the rest of it to Nero?"

"Oh, yes, I suppose so," said the farmer's wife.

So Nero got something to eat after all. And then, when he had fallen asleep in the woodshed where the farmer locked him, the circus men came to take the tame lion back with them.

"I'm very glad to get Nero again," said his trainer. "I guess he has had enough of running away."

And as they were bringing up the new cage which was to take the lion back to the circus, in came Blackie from the meadow where she had been catching grasshoppers.

"Oh, so you did come to see me, after all!" she mewed to Nero.

"Yes," answered the lion, in animal talk, which none of the people could understand, "I came to see you."

"I'm sorry I was away," said Blackie.

"So am I. But I really had a pretty good time," said Nero. "And I scared a man who wore very ragged clothes, something like the funny clowns in our circus. And now I am going back there. I'm glad to have met you, Blackie."

"And I'm glad I met you, Nero. Maybe someday I'll come to your circus."

"Yes, do," growled Nero.

"Good-bye!" called the little girl to the circus lion, as he was hauled away in his cage. "Good-bye! I'm glad you did the sitting-up trick for me!"

Late that afternoon Nero was back in the circus tent again.

"Well, where in the world have you been?" asked Tum Tum.

"Oh, off having adventures, as I suppose you'd call them," answered the lion.

"Adventures!" exclaimed the jolly elephant. "Well, if that man hears about them he'll put you in a book."

"Oh, I guess not," said Nero, as he curled up in his new cage.

But I did, just the same, and here's the book. And so we come to the end of Nero's many adventures—at least for a time. But there are other animals to tell about.

In the circus was a striped tiger, of whom I have spoken. I think I will tell you about him. And so the next volume in this series will be called: "Tamba, the Tame Tiger: His Many Adventures."

And now we will leave Nero peacefully sleeping in his cage, and dreaming, perhaps, of the little girl and Blackie and of the tramp with the boiled ham.

THE END